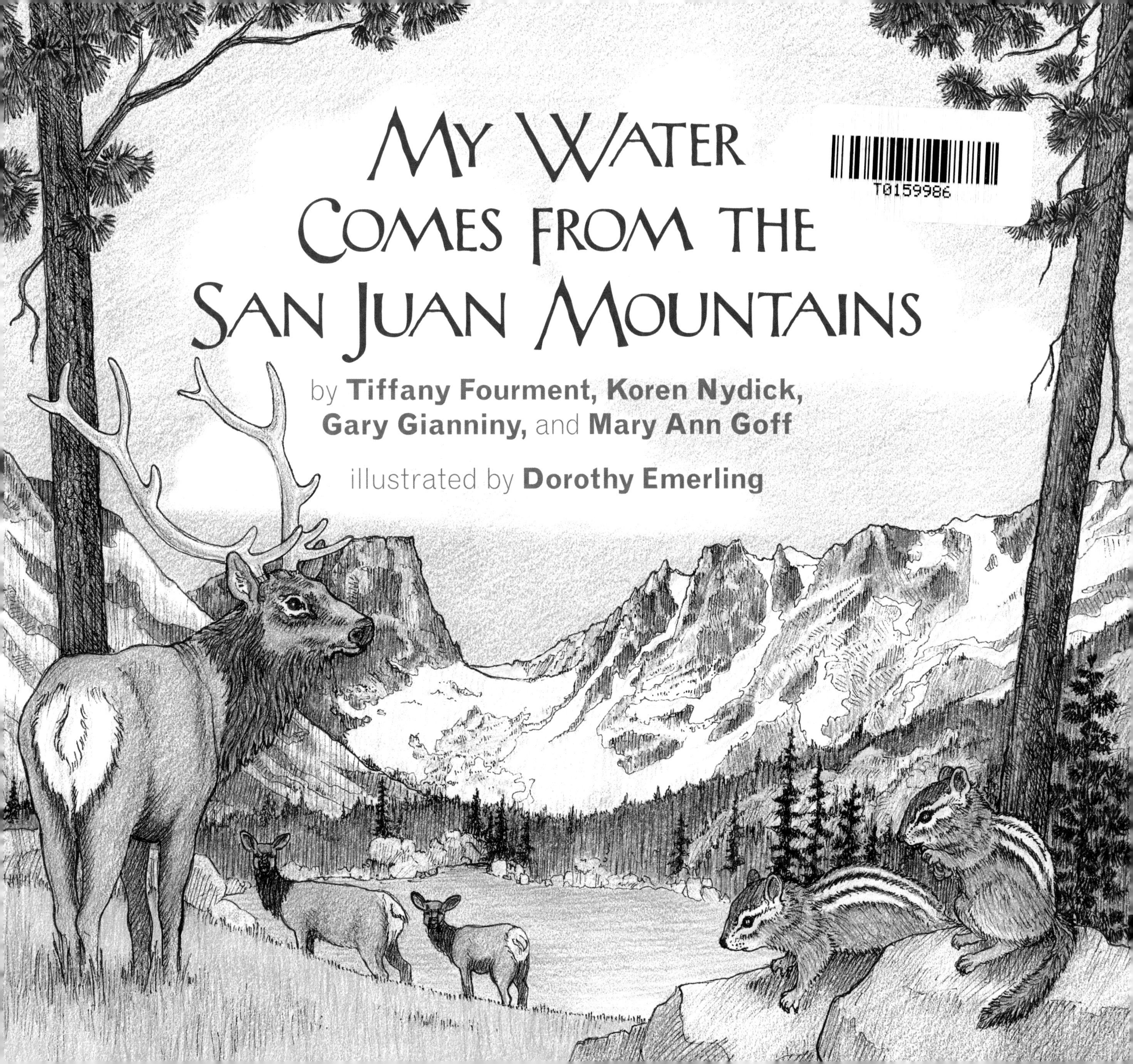

My Water Comes from the San Juan Mountains

by **Tiffany Fourment, Koren Nydick, Gary Gianniny,** and **Mary Ann Goff**

illustrated by **Dorothy Emerling**

This book is a result of the San Juan Collaboratory, which partners the Mountain Studies Institute and Fort Lewis College with the University of Colorado at Boulder. It is an adaptation of an earlier book prepared through the Niwot Ridge Long Term Ecological Research project of the Institute of Arctic and Alpine Research at the University of Colorado, in recognition of the International Year of Mountain. The author, Tiffany Fourment, participated in an alpine ecology field course taught by Prof. Diane McKnight at the Mountain Research Station.

Support for the book was provided by the K-12 Schoolyard Program of the Long Term Ecological Program of the National Science Foundation, University of Colorado at Boulder, Southwestern Water Conservation District, and the Mountain Studies Institute.

Moonlight Publishing LLC
2528 Lexington Street
Lafayette, CO 80026
www.moonlight-publishing.com

Distributed by National Book Network

Library of Congress Cataloging-in-Publication Data applied for

ISBN 13: 978-0-9817700-2-4 (cloth)
ISBN 13: 978-0-9817700-3-1 (paper)

Manufactured in Canada.

Acknowledgements

The book includes text and illustrations contributed by third grade students from Needham Elementary in Durango, Colorado. The publisher, authors, and illustrator would like to thank the following organizations, schools, and individuals for participating in the preparation and funding of this book:

Teacher Laurie True and her students at Needham Elementary School

The San Juan Collaboratory, including the Mountain Studies Institute, Fort Lewis College, and the University of Colorado at Boulder

Organizations

Mountain Studies Institute

Fort Lewis College

Niwot Ridge Long Term Ecological Research Schoolyard program

National Science Foundation

University of Colorado at Boulder Institute of Arctic and Alpine Research

The Southwestern Water Conservation District

Individuals

Dr. Diane McKnight

Dr. Mark Williams

Bruce Whitehead

Robert Blair

Mary Barter

About the Long Term Ecological Research (LTER) Network

The National Science Foundation's LTER network was begun in 1980 and now includes 26 research sites. The goals of the LTER network are:

- Understanding: To understand a diverse array of ecosystems at multiple spatial and temporal scales.
- Synthesis: To create general knowledge through long-term, interdisciplinary research, synthesis of information, and development of theory.
- Information: To inform the LTER and broader scientific community by creating well designed and well documented databases.
- Legacies: To create a legacy of well-designed and documented long-term observations, experiments, and archives of samples and specimens for future generations.
- Education: To promote training, teaching, and learning about long-term ecological research and theEarth's ecosystems, and to educate a new generation of scientists.
- Outreach: To reach out to the broader scientific community, natural resource managers, policymakers, and the general public by providing decision support, information, recommendations and the knowledge and capability to address complex environmental challenges.

"The snow melts and forms little streams that create bigger streams and then bigger streams make rivers."
—Landy

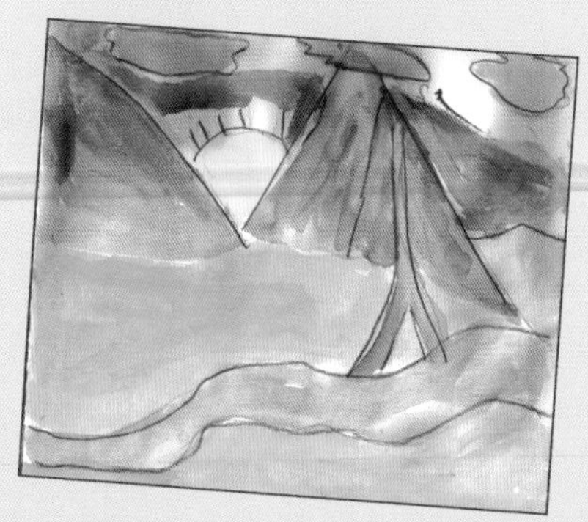

About the San Juan Collaboratory

The University of Colorado at Boulder, Fort Lewis College, Mountain Studies Institute and San Juan Public Lands (USFS/BLM) have developed a new collaborative effort for integrated environmentally based studies on the Western Slope of Colorado. This coordinated effort develops multi-disciplinary, problem-oriented research efforts to serve the needs of rural Southwestern Colorado and establish learning opportunities by building bridges between educational institutions and community groups. See http://sjc.colorado.edu.

About the Mountain Studies Institute and the Southwestern Water Conservation District

The Mountain Studies Institute (MSI) is a highly collaborative, non-advocacy, not-for-profit center for research and education in the San Juan Mountains. MSI's mission is to enhance understanding and sustainable use of the San Juan Mountains and its communities. MSI brings research and planning expertise to the San Juan region and applies the results through education and on-the-ground projects. See www.mountainstudies.org.

The Southwestern Water Conservation District (SWWCD) in southwestern Colorado serves La Plata, Montezuma, Archuleta, San Juan, San Miguel, Dolores and parts of Montrose, Hinsdale and Mineral counties. The SWWCD was created by the State of Colorado to secure and insure an adequate supply of water for the present and future. See http://www.swwcd.org/.

One day, way up in the San Juan Mountains, snow fell softly to the ground.

"What's the big deal about that?" you ask. Snow falls every winter in the San Juan Mountains. But do you know what happens to the snow after it's on the ground? Any guesses? Yes, it melts and turns into water, and that very same snow that falls in those mountains is what comes out of our faucets. When we get a drink of water, take a bath, or turn on the sprinklers in our yard, we are drinking, bathing, and watering our grass with snow.

Sound strange? Well, if you've ever wondered where your water comes from, how it gets to you, or where it goes after we use it, read on, and follow water's journey through a watershed as it changes from the fluffy white snow we see in the mountains to the clear liquid we use every day.

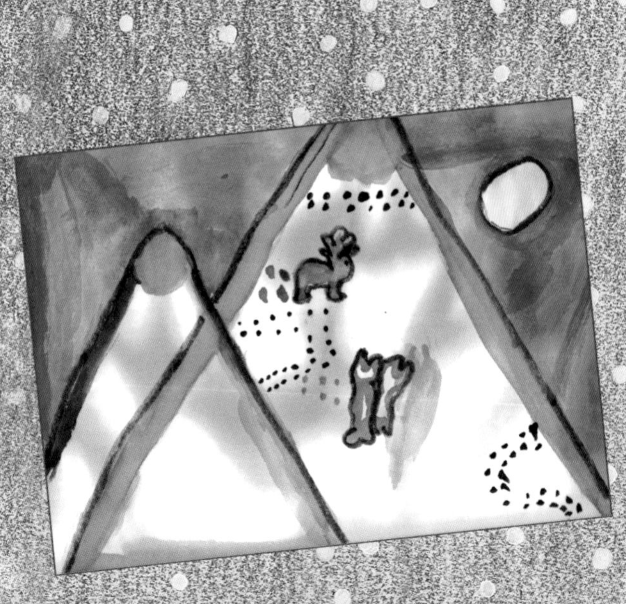

"Snowing with animals in snow."
—Katja

"Snow melts in the mountains and makes the rivers rise. A river runs through my town."
—James

Before we start this journey, though, there is one big question: *What is a watershed*? A **watershed** is an area of land where water collects. The water runs down the mountains and hills, and then drains into creeks or lakes in the valley bottoms. A watershed includes not only the river or lake where the water ends up but also the land that the water flows through. So what does this mean? Well, much like when a dog sheds its hair during the summer, the mountains and hills "shed" water after it snows or rains.

The Continental Divide is a boundary for many watersheds, and the Continental Divide runs through the San Juan Mountains. What watershed do you live in? Well, if you live in the San Juans on the west side of the Continental Divide, you are part of the West Slope Watershed. Your water flows west through New Mexico, Utah, Arizona, Nevada, California, and western Mexico to find its way into the Pacific Ocean in the Sea of Cortez.

If you live in the San Juans east of the Continental Divide, you are part of the East Slope Watershed. Instead of flowing west, water from your watershed runs east and south through New Mexico, Texas, and Mexico to end up all the way down in the Gulf of Mexico, which is a part of the Atlantic Ocean. That's some journey!

Just think — the stream running through your neighborhood is not only the water you drink but eventually the water that much of the western part of the country drinks too. Now that's some big drinking fountain!

"A watershed is when all the creeks flow together. They form a bigger river or even a lake. The San Juan Mountains have lots of rivers like the San Juan, Dolores, Piedra, and La Plata Rivers."

—Ben

"The Continental Divide is where the water flows to one side or the other."

—Steven

All the water on Earth is part of one big cycle, the **water cycle.** The journey of water through your watershed is only a small part of the water cycle. Throughout the whole planet, the sun's heat causes the **evaporation** of water from oceans, lakes, and streams. When water is

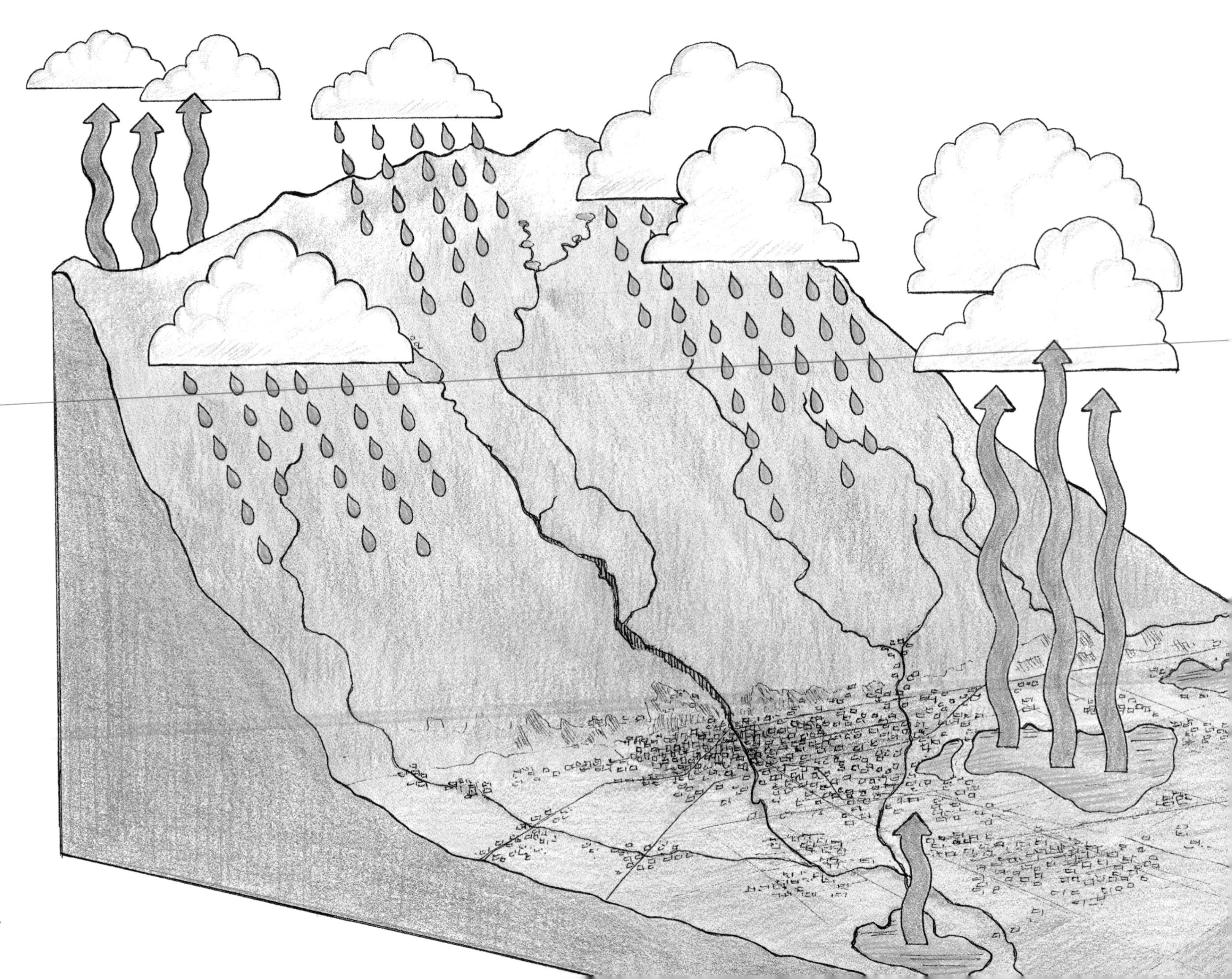

evaporated, it changes from liquid water that you're used to into a gas called **water vapor**. As the warm water vapor rises into the cooler air higher up, **condensation** occurs and clouds are created. When the clouds get heavy with moisture, the water falls back to Earth as **precipitation**. You know precipitation as rain, sleet, and snow. Precipitation collects again in oceans, lakes, or streams that may be far away from where it evaporated in the beginning. Of course, as we will see, water can go through many different stages in its journey, but whether it's vapor or snow or rain, it is always part of Earth's water cycle.

Now that you know a little bit about water and watersheds, let's take a trip through a San Juan Mountain watershed, from the high mountaintops all the way down to the Pacific Ocean.

The Water Cycle

"Water evaporates by the heat of the sun and then the water vapor condenses into clouds and then the water turns to precipitation and rains, hails, sleets or snows onto the mountains. Then it flows into rivers and then back to the ocean and it happens all over again."

—Garrett

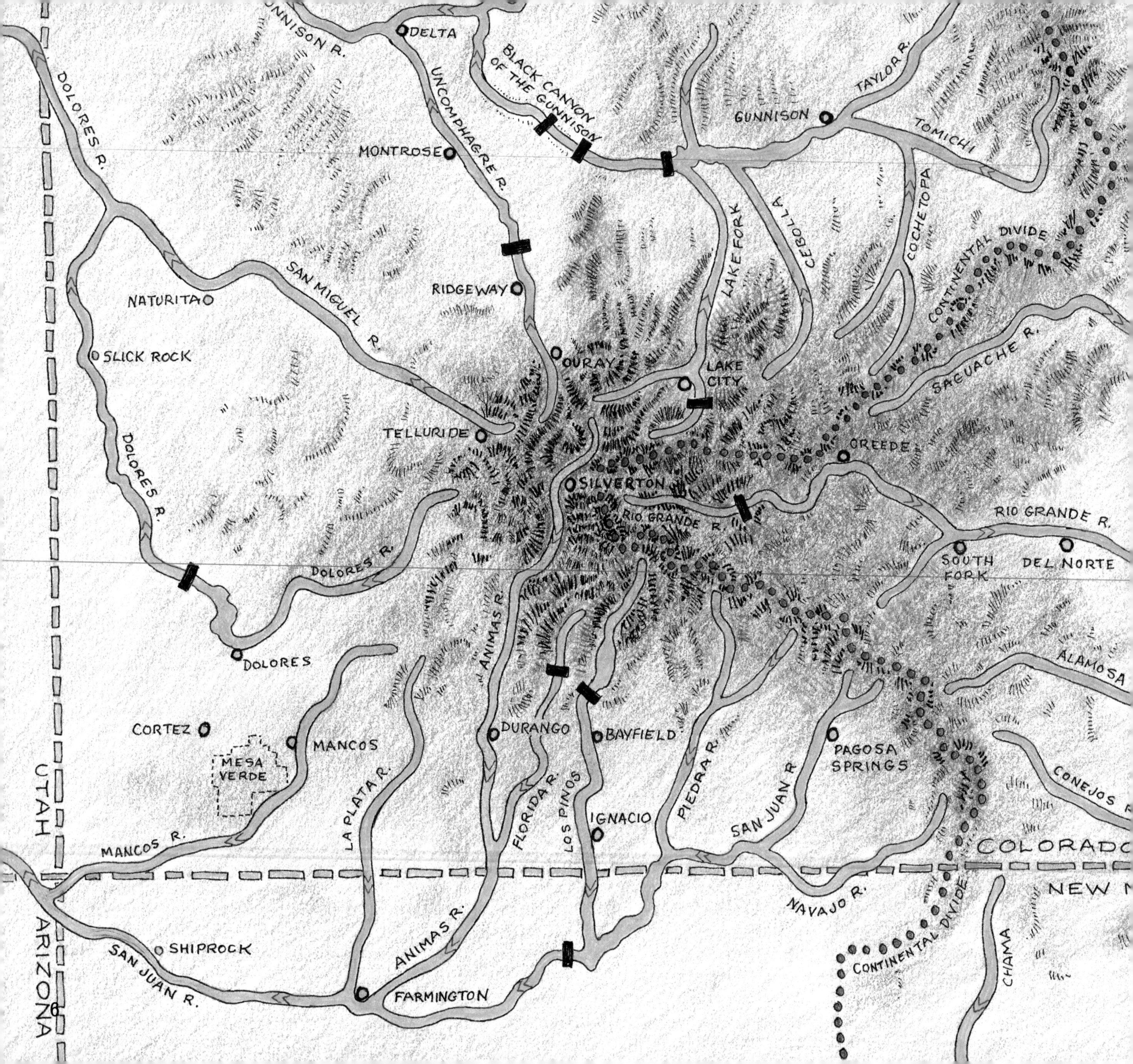

UNNISON R.
DELTA
BLACK CANYON OF THE GUNNISON
UNCOMPHAGRE R.
DOLORES R.
MONTROSE
GUNNISON
TAYLOR R.
TOMICHI
LAKE FORK
CEBOLLA
COCHETOPA
CONTINENTAL DIVIDE
SAN MIGUEL R.
RIDGEWAY
NATURITA
SLICK ROCK
OURAY
LAKE CITY
SAGUACHE R.
TELLURIDE
CREEDE
DOLORES R.
SILVERTON
RIO GRANDE R.
RIO GRANDE R.
SOUTH FORK
DEL NORTE
DOLORES R.
ANIMAS R.
DOLORES
ALAMOSA
CORTEZ
DURANGO
BAYFIELD
MANCOS
MESA VERDE
PAGOSA SPRINGS
LA PLATA R.
FLORIDA R.
LOS PINOS
IGNACIO
PIEDRA R.
SAN JUAN R.
CONEJOS
UTAH
MANCOS R.
COLORADO
NEW M
NAVAJO R.
ARIZONA
CONTINENTAL DIVIDE
SHIPROCK
ANIMAS R.
CHAMA
SAN JUAN R.
FARMINGTON
CONTINENTAL DIVIDE

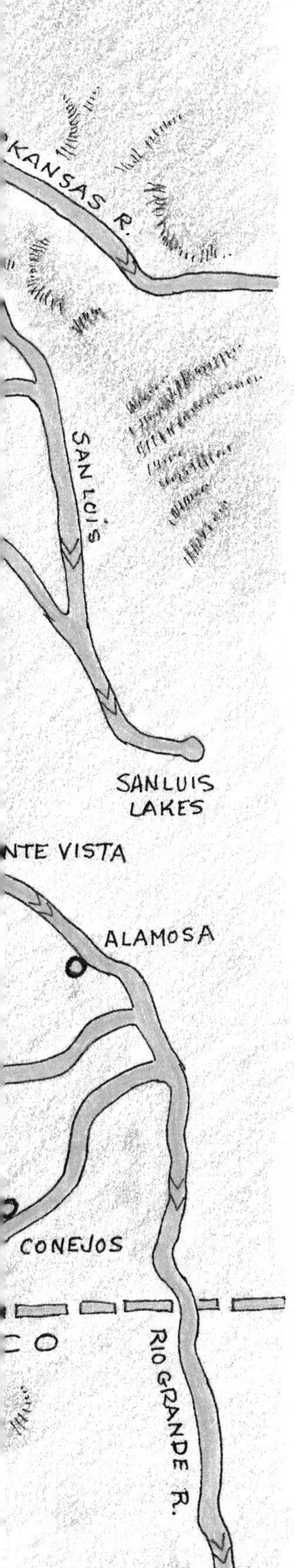

San Juan Watershed

This is a map of the streams and rivers in the San Juan Mountains to help us prepare for our journey. Creeks start high in the mountains and join to form streams and larger rivers in the valleys. The thick black lines on the map represent dams on the rivers. The water caught behind the dams forms reservoirs like Vallecito Reservoir, McPhee Reservoir, Navajo Reservoir, Blue Mesa Reservoir, and Lake San Cristobal.

Can you find the rivers that flow near you? Is there a reservoir near you? Where does your river flow after it goes by your town?

"It rains a lot in the mountains."

—Nichole

The journey of water through our watersheds begins way up in the mountaintops. Here, the snow that falls in the winter collects on the ground and waits for the warm spring sun to melt it. Snow can also collect on snowfields, which are large fields of snow located high in the San Juan Mountains.

Sometimes these areas don't completely melt in the summer, which is why you and I can see snow-covered mountains even in the middle of July.

During the winter, scientists measure how much snow has fallen in the San Juan Mountains. The snow they

Elk

measure is called the snowpack, because as you guessed it, the snow is packed down tight giving the scientists the perfect way to measure how much has accumulated. By checking to see how much water is stored in the snowpack, they can predict the amount of water that will come down from the mountains as snowmelt. The larger the snowpack is, the more water there will be in the streams and rivers in the spring and summer and the more water there will be on the long journey down the mountain.

Chipmunk

Snowfields

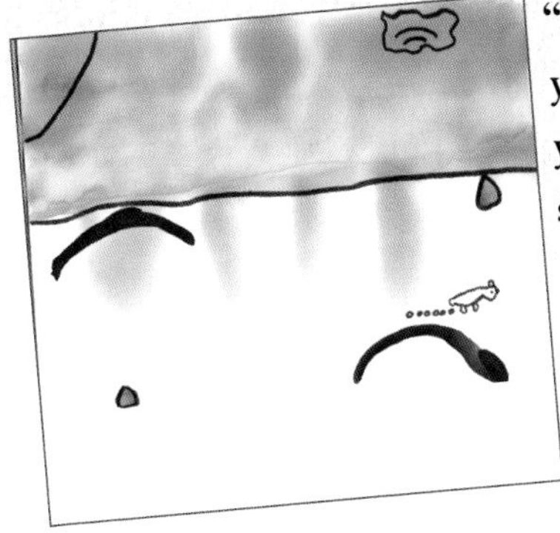

"Sometimes when you get out of town you see big, open snowfields. When the snow is super deep there are bunnies and tree tops that stick out of the ground"

—Kaitlin

Rock Glaciers

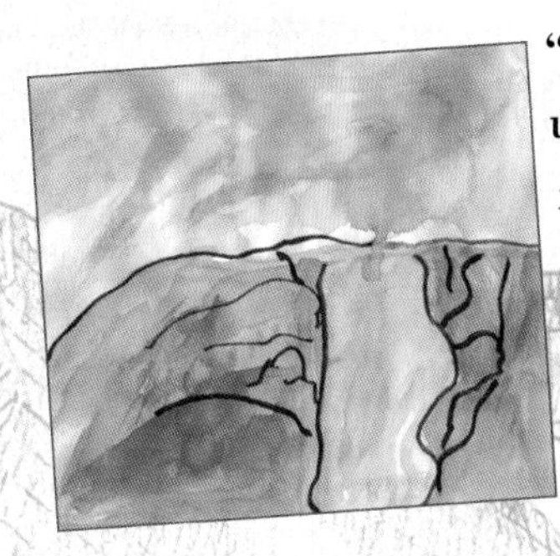

"Rock glaciers are underground glaciers made of rock and ice. Rock glaciers store water underground high in the San Juan Mountains."

—Kiara

Snowmelt

"When spring comes and the sun is warmer the snow from the mountains melts. When snow melts it creates little streams. Then the little streams form into rivers or go into larger rivers. It can melt slowly or it can melt quickly which causes the rivers to overflow."

—Kele

In the spring, the snow starts to melt off the mountaintops from piles of large rocks called **talus**, which are at the very top of the San Juan Mountains. As the snow melts, it trickles downward through an area called the **alpine tundra**, which has many small plants with pretty flowers that bloom in the summer. This is an area that is on the highest part of the mountains and is so cold and windy that only special plants or animals can survive there, ones that do not live anywhere else.

White-tailed ptarmigan

There aren't any tall trees that live in the alpine tundra because the high winds and cold temperatures are too much for them. The tall pine trees that you see every day would just freeze and blow over in this tough climate. The plants that do grow in the alpine tundra are rooted tight into the mountain and grow in small clumps very close to the ground where they are more protected from the wind.

Wind

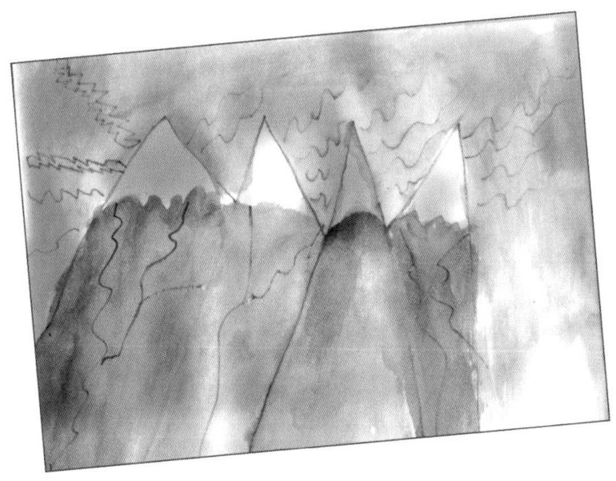

"It can get windy in the mountains. When you climb to the mountain top it is really windy and it feels like you get blown off. "

—Dana

"The San Juan Mountains are very pretty. I really like when the sun reflects the snow on the mountains."

—Peyton

Only a few special animals live in the alpine tundra year-round. They include the yellow-bellied marmot, pika, and white-tailed ptarmigan (pronounced tar-mi-gan). They must have special **adaptations** to help them survive in this cold, windy place. The water that drips and trickles through the rock fields on the alpine tundra is a friendly companion of the pika, a small creature that looks like a chubby squirrel without a long tail. CHEEP CHEEP – As the pika scurries among the rocks, its high-pitched call sounds almost like a bird chirping.

Pika

Yellow-bellied marmot

MARMOTS

"Marmots are like large ground squirrels. They make a loud whistle when they talk to each other. They hibernate in the winter." —Christopher

PIKAS

"Pikas are known as "rock rabbits". They look like little hamsters. Pikas are herbivores, which means that they eat plants and twigs. Pikas like to live in rock crevices." —Caleb

As the water continues downhill from the alpine tundra, it flows through patches of twisted, funny-looking trees that grow close to the ground. These trees, called **krummholz**, grow in very special ways that help them to survive. Because they grow very high up on the sides of the mountains (sometimes over 11,000 feet in elevation), they adapt to this environment by growing sideways with their treetops pointing away from the wind. Branches grow just on the side of the tree that doesn't get hit by the winds. These trees are called **flagged** trees because they look like flags with their branches pointing down wind. Some of these trees are hundreds of years old, and they only come up to your knees! They often mark the **treeline**, which is the highest **altitude** at which trees can grow.

White-crowned Sparrow

Short-tailed weasel

Snowshoe hare

Treeline

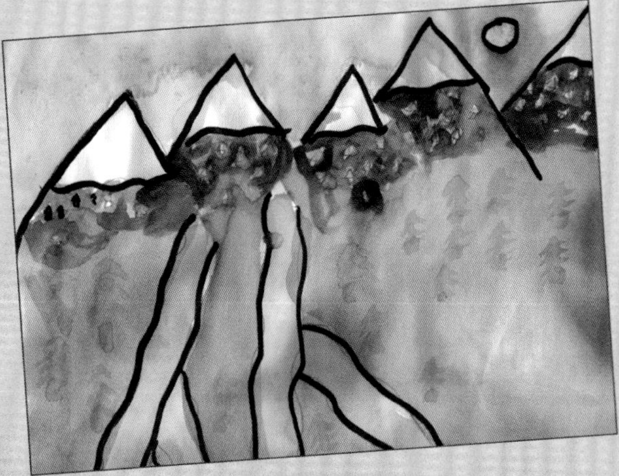

"There are trees on the mountains and one point the trees stop growing. It is usually too high for trees to grow. You can see this at the tippy-top of Engineer Mountain." —Celia

"Treeline is a special place where trees can't grow past. This is very high on the mountains." —Kobe

As the water keeps flowing downward, it enters the **sub-alpine** forest of larger, more "normal-looking" trees. Since they don't live in harsh windy conditions like the krummholz trees, they grow taller and straighter. In this forest, the water that has been trickling along the ground starts to collect in small streams and ponds where animals can take a drink. The sub-alpine **life zone** provides **habitat** for the pine marten, snowshoe hare, the mountain lion, and birds of all shapes and sizes.

Mountain lion

Great horned owl

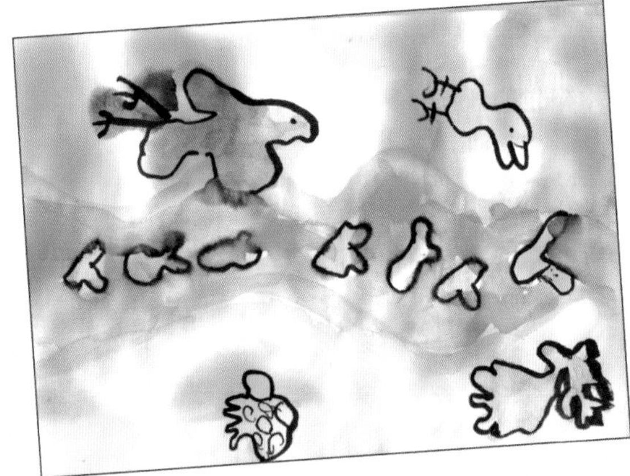

"The plants in the San Juans are mainly trees. There are also lots of animals that live here like fish, eagles, elk, bear, and moose."

—Eric

LYNX

"Lynx have really big feet to help them walk in the snow. They love to eat snowshoe hares. Lynx have recently been reintroduced to the San Juan Mountains. "

—Eric and Kaitlin

From these small streams and ponds, the water starts to flow into larger streams and ponds as it moves down the mountains. Some streams flow into **reservoirs.** These are large, human-made lakes with a dam at one end that traps and stores the water until it is needed. Dams are large structures that act as gates to control the flow of water.

Some of the water released by the dam flows into even larger streams. From there, some water flows into ditches or canals

where the water is stored again until someone needs to use it, often for watering crops. Some water released by the dam makes its way into pipes that take it to a water treatment facility, or "plant," where it is cleaned to make it safe for people to drink. Finally, any extra released water flows into streams throughout the watershed.

Lakes and reservoirs

"A reservoir is a lake and there is a dam to stop the water. These dams help give us water to drink and make lakes to go fishing on. Reservoirs are man made lake." —Colton

"This guy likes to ride his boat on Pagosa Lake. He likes to fish." — Riley

Mule deer

Water can flow through several types of landforms as it heads down the mountains. Sometimes the water pours and splashes over waterfalls with a crashing ROAR. Creeks also flow through mountain meadows and rush through steep canyons.

Below the sub-alpine life zone, we enter the **montane** life zone. Many plants and animals such as fox, coyotes, and chipmunks live in this area. They depend on the creeks and streams for food, water, and shelter. Oh look! A deer that has been grazing nearby has gone down to the water for a drink.

Red fox

"Waterfalls are a great place for plants to grow and sometimes fish like to play in the waterfall too."

—Levi

"Trout live in clean rivers and lakes of the San Juan Mountains. The state fish of Colorado is the Colorado River Cutthroat Trout."

—Kele

Gray squirrel
Mallard ducks

"Silverton, Durango, Pagosa Springs and Ouray are all towns that are by rivers. Sometimes living too close to the rivers causes lots of pollution."

—Celia

As the streams of the West Slope leave the San Juan Mountains, they flow through many towns and cities. If you live here, you will often notice that the banks of these streams are lined with cottonwoods. These are the trees that release their seeds in little fluffy tufts of "cotton" that we see floating through the air in the spring.

It's hard for many plants to grow in the cold, dry climate of the mountains. But many types of trees grow well along the streams because their roots get plenty of water. Along with cottonwood you'll find aspen, pine, cedar, and juniper trees growing near streams. The plants, animals, and people living nearby all share the water that flows past them down the mountainside.

"Towns are next to rivers so people can fish a lot and get clean water."

—Kobe

Now remember the water that was piped into the treatment facility from the streams and reservoirs? Well, that water has been treated to make it clean for us to drink and now comes out of our faucets and hoses. If you live in a town (like Durango, Telluride, Bayfield, Cortez or Pagosa Springs) you use this water to drink, bathe, wash dishes, clean clothes, water gardens, and many other things. Think about all the times you use water during the day!

If you live outside of a town or city, you may get water from a different source. Did you know that some water collects under the ground? No surprise, it's called **groundwater.** Groundwater collects under the soil in the spaces between rocks, sand, and gravel. Your water may come from a well that goes underground to collect groundwater deep in the soil. Some groundwater comes from "leaks" in nearby rivers or lakes. But most groundwater comes from the rain and melted snow that trickles down through the soil. Where do you get your water from?

Where Does it Go?

When you drain the bathwater out of your tub, what happens to it? Water that we use in our toilets, sinks, and showers ends up in deep underground in pipes called sanitary sewers. This water flows to a different kind of treatment facility where it is cleaned and released back into the streams and rivers. Some water, like the water that runs down the sides of the street after a big rain, runs directly into the streams through storm drains. This water hasn't been cleaned by a treatment facility, so it's important not to dump oil and other pollutants into storm drains. If that happened, plants and animals would become sick, because this is the water they rely on.

If you live outside of a town or city, there may not be any sanitary sewers or storm drains. The water you use in your house may drain into a septic system, which is buried somewhere under your lawn. Similar to a water treatment facility, a septic system cleans the water before it goes back into the soil as groundwater or into streams.

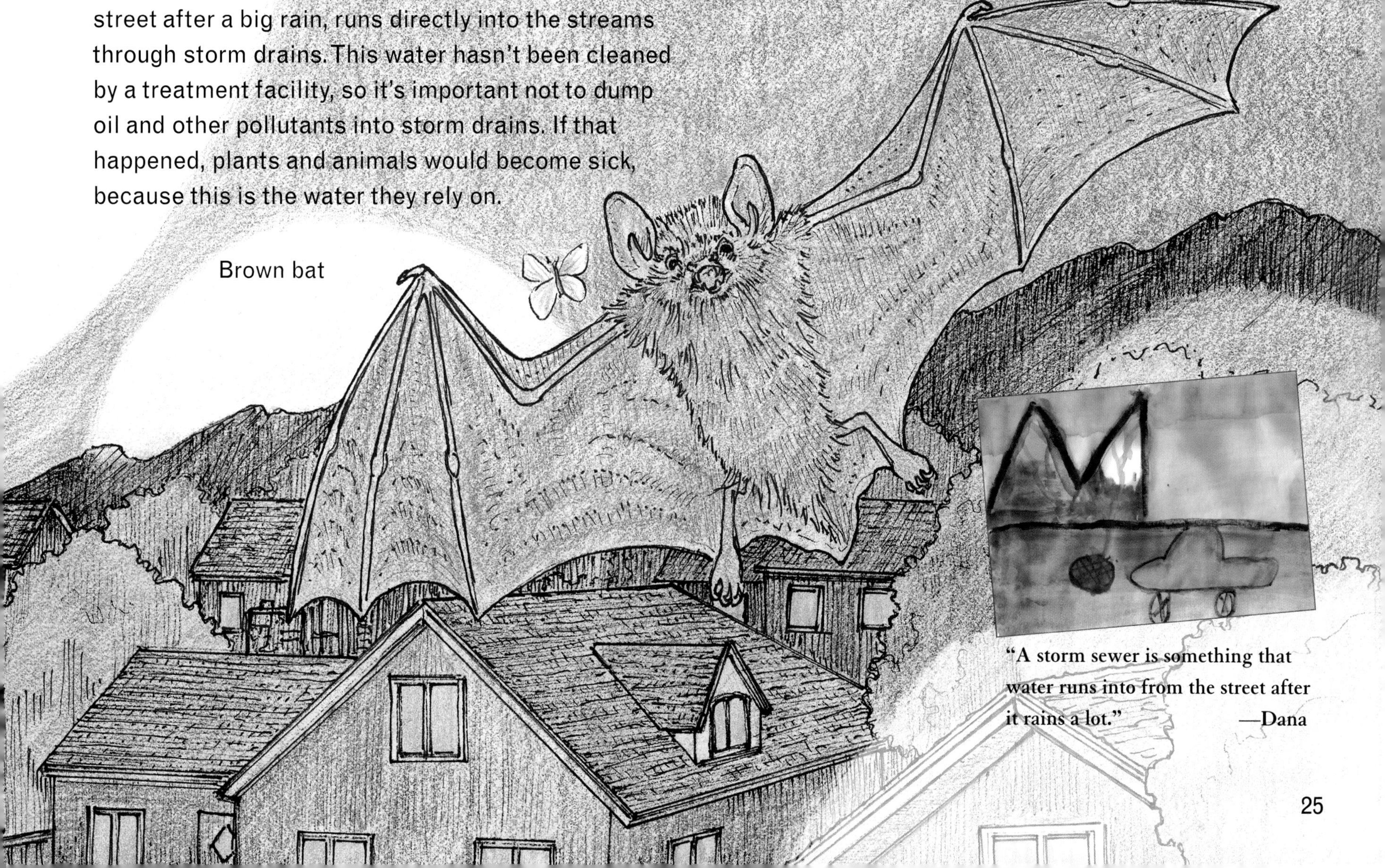

Brown bat

"A storm sewer is something that water runs into from the street after it rains a lot." —Dana

Farmers and ranchers on all sides of the San Juan Mountains provide us with food In these dry regions, some farmers and ranchers depend on reservoirs to irrigate their crops and feed their livestock. To **irrigate** means to supply land or crops with extra water that is needed for the plants to grow. The corn that you buy at a local farmers' market might have been grown with water from the very same creek that flows into your faucets!

Western blue bird

Some farmers use fertilizers to help their crops grow faster and pesticides to keep bugs from eating their crops. These chemicals can dissolve into irrigation water, and this water could get back into the streams and rivers. In towns and cities, pollutants from lawn chemicals or runoff from roads can get into the streams. And unfortunately, when pollution of any sort gets into our streams, it could get into our water supply.

IRRIGATION

"There are farms next to the rivers so the plants can grab the water through their roots and through irrigation systems."

—Aryanna

An **aquifer** is an underground layer of rock and gravel that contains the groundwater. Aquifers can be small, or they can cover hundreds of square miles like the Ogallala Aquifer. This aquifer is so big it lies beneath parts of Wyoming, Colorado, Nebraska, Kansas, Oklahoma, New Mexico, Texas, and South Dakota. Wow! Now that's a lot of water! Much of the water that flows east from the San Juan Mountains is stored underground in a large aquifer under the San Luis Valley. It's then used later for many purposes including drinking water and irrigation.

Many people rely on groundwater. For example, farmers may rely on groundwater that they pump out of the ground to irrigate their crops, and many cities and rural households dig wells to use groundwater for drinking, washing, and bathing. What do you use water for?

"People need to take care of the rivers. Pick up trash!"

—Trinity

Raccoon

Rivers from the San Juan Mountains carry water to people in many downstream states before they reach the ocean. So even though we think of the rivers in our county or town as ours, we are sharing this water with millions of other people. We have a big responsibility to provide them with enough water and to keep that water clean!

On the West Slope of the San Juan Mountains, the Uncompahgre, San Miguel, Dolores, San Juan, Pine, and Animas Rivers eventually flow into a big river called the Colorado River. The Colorado River carries the water west until it lands in the Pacific Ocean.

There is one river in the San Juan Mountains that flows toward the Gulf of Mexico in the Atlantic Ocean. It's called the Rio Grande. It starts in the mountains at the top of Wolf Creek Pass above the town of Creede. Farther north in the Rocky Mountains, there are many East Slope streams that flow into big rivers such as the Platte, Arkansas, and Missouri Rivers. Most of this water goes to the Mississippi River and eventually ends up in the Gulf of Mexico, too.

It's a long journey from the mountaintops to the sea, with so much happening along the way. And you're right in the middle of it all.

So what happens when the water finally gets to one of the oceans? That's right! As the sun rises in the sky to warm the new day, the water cycle starts over. Some of the water evaporates out of the ocean, condenses into big fluffy clouds, and eventually, when it gets cold enough, falls as snow. And way up in the San Juan Mountains and in your backyard, snow falls softly to the ground, and the journey begins again.

"Streams join into rivers and make bigger rivers and then they go to the ocean. An example is Lightner Creek runs into the Animas River in Durango."

—Kaitlin and Celia

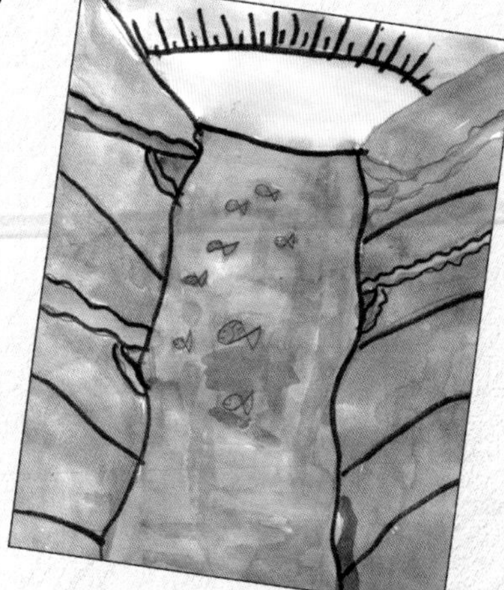